DC SUPER-PETS!

STREAKY!

The Origin of Supergirl's Cat

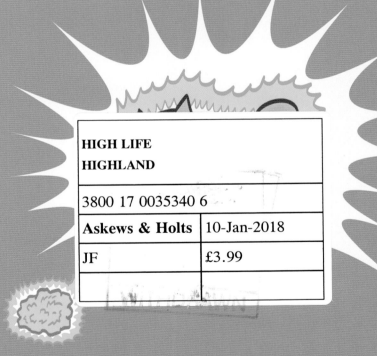

by Steve Korté
illustrated by Art Baltazar
Supergirl created by Jerry Siegel and Joe Shuster
by special arrangement with the Jerry Siegel family

 raintree

a Capstone company — publishers for children

EVERY SUPER HERO NEEDS A
SUPER-PET!

Even Supergirl!
In this origin story, discover
how Streaky the Super-Cat
became the Girl of Steel's
feline friend . . .

One night, a meteor shower lights the sky above the town of Midvale.

WHOOSH!

Supergirl soars through the air. She makes sure no one is harmed.

Then the hero spots a green rock among the meteors. **"Kryptonite!"** she cries. **"My only weakness!"**

The Kryptonite is smaller than a tennis ball but still dangerous.

"Only lead can protect me from the radioactive rock!" the hero says.

Supergirl finds a lead pipe at a nearby construction site. She wraps the pipe around the Kryptonite.

Supergirl decides to experiment on the rock. She hopes to find a cure for its harmful effects.

Supergirl blasts the Kryptonite with her heat vision! Then she freezes it with her super-breath!

Nothing works, so Supergirl throws the Kryptonite deep into a forest.

Later, Supergirl flies over Midvale. With her super-hearing, she notices the sound of two animals fighting.

"Bark! Bark!" In an alley, a big brown dog growls at a small orange cat.

Supergirl quickly inhales. *FWOOSH!*

The hero's powerful breath pulls the dog away from the cat. The canine bully flees in fear.

"Miaow!" the cat cries up at Supergirl.

WHOOSH!

The super hero swoops down and picks up the friendly feline.

"I'm going to adopt you," Supergirl says. She admires the two yellow streaks of fur on the cat's sides. **"And I will call you . . . Streaky!"**

Days later, Streaky wanders into the forest. The curious cat sniffs a small green rock on the ground.

The Kryptonite!

A bright glow surrounds Streaky's body. He floats into the air.

"What's happening?" wonders the cat. "I . . . I can fly!"

Supergirl's experiments have changed the Kryptonite into a new material.

The X-Kryptonite gives Streaky superpowers!

"I'm a Super-Cat!" cries Streaky as he soars through the air. "I bet there's nothing I can't do!"

FWOOSH! Streaky rockets above Midvale. Below, six cats stare sadly at a milk lorry.

"Those cats look hungry!" says Streaky.

Streaky zips under the lorry and pushes it up into the air. Milk bottles fall to the ground and spill onto the pavement.

"MIAOW! MIAOW!"

The happy cats lap up the sweet drink.

Then Streaky the Super-Cat searches for other cats to help.

Suddenly, he comes face-to-face with a mighty foe: **another dog!**

"Well, well," says the angry dog. **"Who will save you?"**

FWOOP! Streaky jumps onto the limb of a nearby apple tree.

The angry dog barks at Streaky. "Come down, you coward!"

"Hey, wait a minute," Streaky thinks aloud. "What am I afraid of? I'm the mightiest cat in the world!"

With super-strength, he shakes the tree. Lots of apples fall on top of the dog.

"How do you like those apples, you big bully?" Streaky calls down.

"Stop it!" cries the dog as he flees.

The Super-Cat lets loose with a deafening, "MIIIAAAOOWWWW!"

His voice booms like thunder.

Many kilometres away, the ear-splitting sound awakens Supergirl.

"That's Streaky's miaow!" she says, worried. "What on Earth is going on?"

FWOOSH! Supergirl flies through the sky in search of her feline friend.

Nearby, Streaky zooms above a farm.

He spots a hawk attacking baby chicks.

"Think you're tough?" Streaky says.

"Peck on someone your own size!"

BLAM-O!!

Streaky slams into the hawk in mid-air.

The hawk quickly flies away.

Supergirl arrives just in time to see

Streaky save the chicks.

"What a wonderful surprise!" says Supergirl. "Let's have some fun together!"

The hero picks up a heavy spool of copper wire and throws it into the air.

FWOOSH!

Streaky rockets through the sky, pouncing on the spool like a ball of wool. Soon, he is tangled up in the wire.

"HA!" Supergirl laughs with delight.

Suddenly, Streaky loses his powers and starts to fall!

"I feel . . . weak!" the Super-Cat thinks. "What's happening?"

WHOOSH! Supergirl soars over to Streaky and gathers him in her arms.

"Don't worry, Streaky," she says. "I'll save you!"

Afterwards, Streaky returns to his life as an ordinary cat.

"I wonder what gave Streaky superpowers," Supergirl thinks. **"Will he ever be a Super-Cat again?"**

Weeks later, Streaky playfully chases a ball of wool back into the forest.

The curious cat once again stumbles upon the X-Kryptonite.

"Help! Help!" Streaky hears.

His super-hearing – and other powers – are back!

Streaky looks up. Above him, a hot-air balloon falls through the sky.

"Save us!" shout the people in the basket.

Streaky zooms **up, up and away!**

He gathers the balloon's ropes in his mouth and sets the basket on the ground.

"Thank you, Super-Cat!" says a grateful man.

Supergirl welcomes the return of her Super-Pet. She introduces Streaky to **Superman's dog, Krypto!**

The two amazing animals become great friends and enjoy playing together. A tug-of-war competition lasts for hours!

Finally, Supergirl declares that both Super-Pets are winners!

Alongside Krypto, Streaky teams up with a group of heroic animals, known as **the Legion of Super-Pets.**

Streaky proudly takes his place at the team's headquarters. He joins forces with Beppo the Super-Monkey, Comet the Super-Horse and others.

The mighty members fight evildoers and protect people and animals around the world.

Most of all, Streaky loves spending time with Supergirl.

When two lions escape from the African Safari exhibit at the Midvale Zoo, he and Supergirl team up to save the day!

FWOOSH! Supergirl swoops in to take the frightened zoo visitors to safety.

"MIAOW!" Streaky chases the lions back to their cages.

After a long day, Streaky curls up in Supergirl's lap near a warm fireplace.

"PURRRRRR!" The Super-Pet's thunderous purring fills the room.

"They say a dog is a human's best friend," Supergirl says, as she gently rubs her fingers behind Streaky's ears. **"But a Super-Cat is my best friend!"**

STREAKY!

REAL NAME:
Streaky

SPECIES:
Domestic shorthair
super-cat

BIRTHPLACE:
Midvale

HEIGHT:
23 centimetres

WEIGHT:
4.3 kilograms

Super hero owner:
SUPERGIRL

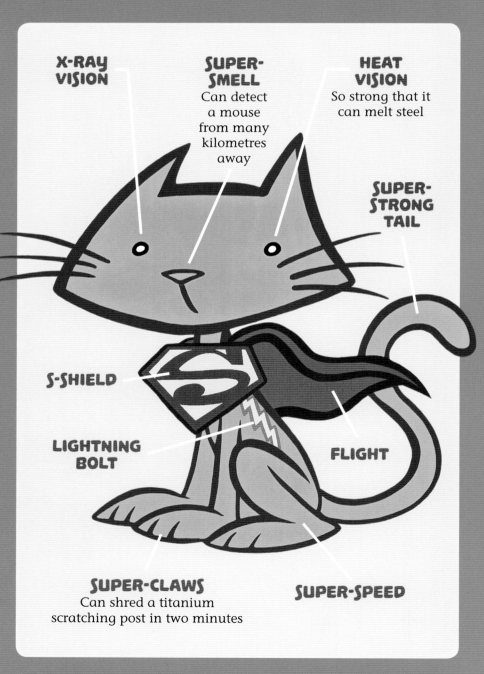

X-RAY VISION

SUPER-SMELL
Can detect a mouse from many kilometres away

HEAT VISION
So strong that it can melt steel

SUPER-STRONG TAIL

S-SHIELD

LIGHTNING BOLT

FLIGHT

SUPER-CLAWS
Can shred a titanium scratching post in two minutes

SUPER-SPEED

HERO PET PALS!

COMET

Super hero owner:
SUPERGIRL

KRYPTO

Super hero owner:
SUPERMAN

FUZZY

Super hero owner:
SUPERBOY

WHIZZY

Super hero owner:
SUN BOY

STINKY

Super hero owner:
POWER GIRL

STEEL
TURTLE

Super hero owner:
STEEL

VILLAIN PET FOES!

BIZARRO
STREAKY

Super-villain owner:
BIZARRO

BRAINICAT

Super-villain owner:
BRAINIAC

GENERAL
MANX

Super-villain owner:
GENERAL ZOD

NOVA

Super-villain owner:
TERRA MAN

MECHANIKAT

Super-villain owner:
METALLO

IGNATIUS

Super-villain owner:
LEX LUTHOR

STREAKY JOKES!

What is a cat's
favourite colour?
Purr-ple!

What did the cat have
for breakfast?
Mice Krispies!

What kind of cats like
to go bowling?
Alley cats!

GLOSSARY!

admire look at something and enjoy it

coward someone who is easily scared and runs away from frightening situations

curious eager to find out

Kryptonite radioactive rock from Krypton that weakens Supergirl and Superman

lead soft, grey metal

meteor piece of rock from space that enters Earth's atmosphere, burns and forms a streak of light in the sky

radioactive material that gives off harmful particles as it breaks down

READ THEM ALL!

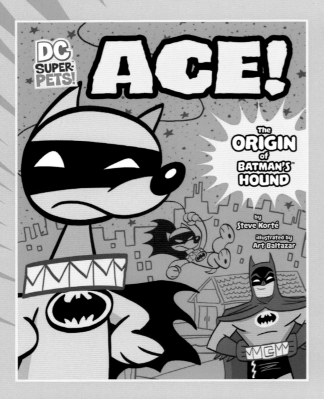

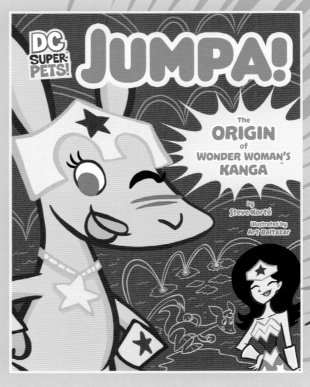

HERE IS ANOTHER STORY ABOUT ME!

DC SUPER-PETS!™

AUTHOR!

Steve Korté is the author of many books for children and young adults. He worked at DC Comics for many years, editing more than 600 books about Superman, Batman, Wonder Woman and the other heroes and villains in the DC Universe. He lives in New York, USA, with his own super-cat, Duke.

ILLUSTRATOR!

Famous cartoonist Art Baltazar is the creative force behind *The New York Times* bestselling, Eisner Award-winning DC Comics' Tiny Titans; co-writer for Billy Batson and the Magic of Shazam, Young Justice, Green Lantern Animated (Comic); and artist/co-writer for the Tiny Titans/ Little Archie crossover, Superman Family Adventures, Super Powers and Itty Bitty Hellboy! Art is one of the founders of Aw Yeah Comics. He stays at home and draws comics and never has to leave the house! He lives with his lovely wife, Rose, sons Sonny and Gordon, and daughter Audrey. Visit him at www.artbaltazar.com